BUGGED!

by Michelle Knudsen
illustrated by Blanche Sims

Kane Press, Inc.
New York

To Jonah, Kristi, Stephanie and Andrew—Love, B. S.

Library of Congress Cataloging-in-Publication Data

Knudsen, Michelle.
  Bugged! / by Michelle Knudsen ; illustrated by Blanche Sims.
    p. cm. — (Science solves it!)
  "Life Science/Mosquitoes-Grades: 1/3."
  Summary: Tired of being covered in itchy mosquito bites, Riley uses science to investigate
why mosquitoes are more attracted to him than to his friends.
  ISBN-13: 978-1-57565-259-7 (alk. paper)
  [1. Mosquitoes—Fiction. 2. Bites and stings—Fiction.] I. Sims, Blanche, ill. II. Title.
  PZ7.K7835Bu 2008
  [E]—dc22
                              2007026567

10 9 8 7 6 5 4 3 2 1

First published in the United States of America in 2008 by Kane Press, Inc.
Printed in Hong Kong.

Science Solves It! is a registered trademark of Kane Press, Inc.

www.kanepress.com

It's summer. It's Saturday. I'm having an awesome time hanging out with my friends, until—

BZZZZZZZZZZZZ!

Oh, no.

They've found me.

I dance around, flinging my arms and legs like crazy. "Shoo! Go away!" But it's no use. One bites me on the ankle. Another bites my elbow. I look ridiculous, but I keep on dancing.

"Your buddies are back, Riley," says Lara.

"Here, I'll help you drive them off," Steve says. "What are friends for?" He starts doing the mosquito dance with me.

We all laugh. But really, it's not that funny. It's been like this for weeks. The mosquitoes are out to get me.

Mosquito is Spanish for "little fly." Mosquitoes are a kind of insect. They've been around for hundreds of millions of years! There are about 2,700 different types of mosquitoes in the world.

Soon I'm covered with itchy bites. Steve
points to a tiny bump on his elbow. "Look," he
says. "They got me, too."

"*One* got you," I tell him. "They *all* got me."

"You *have* tried bug spray, right?" asks Lara.

"Can't," I tell her. "Mom doesn't like me to use
stuff with chemicals. Are you guys wearing any?"

"Nope, don't usually need it," says Steve.

"I don't get it," I say. "Why do mosquitoes bother me more than you?"

Lara thinks for a second. "Maybe they like the soap you use. You can try a bar of mine."

"I'll lend you my shampoo," says Steve. They race home and come back with their shower stuff. "What are friends for?" pants Steve.

Did you know that only female mosquitoes bite? They need the blood to help make their eggs. When a mosquito "bites" you, she's actually sticking her proboscis (pruh•bahs•is)—a long, sharp, skinny part of her mouth—into your skin.

I zip home to shower and wash my hair. Then I brave the park at dusk for a game of catch.

BZZZZZZZZZZZ!

No luck! The mosquitoes still have me for dinner.

Most mosquitoes are out and about at dawn and dusk, looking for someone to bite. They're pretty slow flyers— but they beat their wings very fast (300 to 600 times per second!).

The carbon dioxide that people and animals breathe out is one of the main things that attracts mosquitoes. They can sense it from 90 feet away! When they get closer, they can also sense body odor and heat.

THE BITE SITE!

There must be a reason why the mosquitoes are hunting me down. I decide to look online.

"Mosquitoes are attracted to heat, sweat, and the air you breathe out," I read.

Great. So all I need to do is not get hot or sweaty—and stop breathing.

The next day I watch Steve and Lara carefully. They're sweating. They're breathing. But the bugs don't bug them. What am I doing wrong?

I try doing exactly what my friends do. When Lara jumps, I jump. When Steve runs, I run.

BZZZZZZZZZZZ!

It doesn't help.

Later I lie on my bed flipping through a magazine. The mosquito bites are itching like crazy. I try very hard not to scratch.

Then I see something that might solve all my problems!

EZ-Bug-Banisher!
Super Mosquito
effective repellent!
All-Natural Ingredients!

If you get bitten, try not to scratch. The bite could get infected and feel even worse! Just wash it with mild soap and water and put on some calamine lotion or cortisone cream.

I race downstairs. "Mom!" I shout. "Look at this!" I show her the ad. "This stuff is all-natural. Can we order some? Please? Please? *Pleeeease?*"

She reads the whole ad, even the tiny print. Finally she says, "Okay, Riley. Let's give it a try."

Bug repellents containing DEET or Picaridin have been proven to keep mosquitoes away. Some natural bug repellents also work—like products made from the Australian lemon-scented gum tree!

The package arrives a few days later. I tear off the wrapper and rub the EZ-Bug-Banisher all over my arms and legs. I even put some in my hair. This goop had better do the trick! I run off to meet my friends.

"Ugh!" Lara exclaims. "What's that smell?"

Steve sniffs around. "It's *you*, Riley!" he says. "What *is* that?"

I tell them about the ad. They agree to put up with the smell in the interest of science.

"Anything that stinky has to work," says Steve.

When a mosquito "bites," she injects her spit into you! The spit makes it easier for the mosquito to suck your blood. It's actually the spit that makes your skin red and itchy!

At first I'm hopeful. But then—
BZZZZZZZZZZZ!
"Ouch!" I slap at a mosquito that bit me.
"It's not working?" asks Lara.
"Nope," I say, starting my mosquito dance. "In fact, I think they like it!"
Steve starts to laugh. "They're not the only ones." He points behind me.

More cats than I can count are edging closer and closer. They start rubbing up against my legs and purring.

"Great," I groan. "Just great."

Steve and Lara can't stop giggling.

I head home.

Mom thinks the cat parade is pretty funny, too.

"Well, here's one good thing," she says. "You found Furball! Your dad's been looking for him all day."

I sigh. "Glad I could help."

Time for a new plan. I try covering up every inch of my body so the mosquitoes can't get me. I last for two minutes.

One website said that fans can help keep mosquitoes away. But they seem to keep friends away, too!

Solving my mosquito problem is going to take some serious research. We hit the library. There's tons of stuff on insects.

FUN STUFF ABOUT MOSQUITOES

- The buzzing sound a mosquito makes comes from its wings beating really fast.
- Mosquitoes seem to like biting women more than men.
- Beware the full moon! Mosquitoes may be more active when the moon is full.
- One kind of mosquito will travel up to 40 miles just for a meal!

A mosquito's buzz may sound annoying to you—but not to other mosquitoes! Scientists think it helps male mosquitoes find female ones.

Lara holds up a book.
"You could get a pet bat.
Bats eat mosquitoes!"

"Or you could move to Antarctica," says Steve.
"That's the only continent where mosquitoes
don't live."

I'm not that desperate . . . *yet*.

Bats sometimes feed
on mosquitoes. So do
fish, frogs, birds,
and dragonflies.

"Oh, and don't eat Limburger cheese!" says Lara. "This book says mosquitoes are drawn to the smell."

"Ugh," I say. "No problem there. I hate Limburger! Whenever my dad eats it, Mom and I have to leave the room."

I trudge home feeling pretty miserable.
None of these ideas is going to fix my problem.
But early the next morning the phone rings.
"Good news!" says Lara. "My mom's cousin
is a professor at the community college. He's
an expert on bugs! Maybe he can help you."
"Great. The sooner, the better," I say.

"Come in, come in!" Professor Hayes shakes our hands. Several times. I don't think he gets a lot of visitors. His office is filled with bug books and bug pictures and even a box of dead bugs.

"Don't worry," he says, "you're not *bugging* me. Get it? *Bugging* me?" He chuckles. Lara rolls her eyes. I explain my mosquito problem.

"Well," says the professor, "the truth is, some people smell better to mosquitoes. It's just something you're born with."

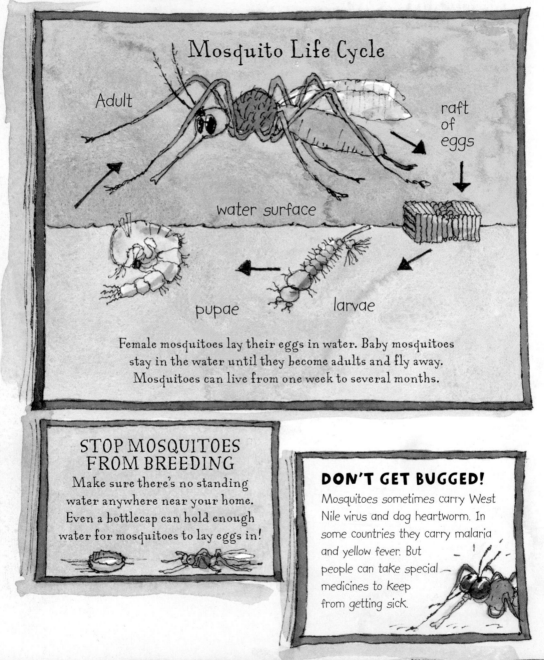

Mosquito Life Cycle

Adult

raft of eggs

water surface

pupae

larvae

Female mosquitoes lay their eggs in water. Baby mosquitoes stay in the water until they become adults and fly away. Mosquitoes can live from one week to several months.

STOP MOSQUITOES FROM BREEDING
Make sure there's no standing water anywhere near your home. Even a bottlecap can hold enough water for mosquitoes to lay eggs in!

DON'T GET BUGGED!
Mosquitoes sometimes carry West Nile virus and dog heartworm. In some countries they carry malaria and yellow fever. But people can take special medicines to keep from getting sick.

"But they're driving me crazy!" I say.

"Making you *bug out*, you mean. Get it? Bug out?" He chuckles again.

Then he adds, "Seriously, though, there are some things you can try." He hands me a list.

DO

- wear antiperspirant (to help you not sweat)
- wear loose-fitting clothes, light colors, and long sleeves and pants
- get rid of standing water near your house— that means changing the water in birdbaths, wading pools, and even your pet's water bowl!

DON'T

- wear perfume or use flowery-smelling products
- hang around in sweaty clothes
- leave torn window screens unrepaired
- go out at dawn or dusk—when mosquitoes are most likely to be out there waiting for you!

We go back to my house. There's a note from Mom: FLOOR CLEAN. SHOES OFF!

We kick off our sneakers. "You guys want a snack?" I open the fridge.

"Ugh!" Lara says. "What's that smell?"

"Eww," says Steve. "Must be your dad's Limburger cheese!"

"Nope," I say. "He ate it all last night."

Steve starts sniffing around like a bloodhound. "It's not coming from the fridge," he says. "I think it's coming from . . . your sneakers."

"And, um, from your feet," adds Lara, holding her nose.

My *sneakers*? My *feet*? I take a big sniff. Hmm. Maybe they are a little smelly.

"Riley," says Lara. "Those are just awful!"

"No offense," adds Steve, "but you need that spray stuff for stinky shoes. Pronto!"

I'm not offended. I'm too busy thinking.

"Did you say Limburger . . . ?" I ask.

I run to my room and grab one of the library books. "Mosquitoes like the smell of Limburger cheese! Remember? It was in this book!"

"You mean . . . all this time, the bugs have been attracted to your *sneakers?*" asks Lara.

"I guess Limburger and stinky sneakers must smell the same to mosquitoes," I say.

Scientists have proven that mosquitoes are attracted to Limburger cheese. And it does sort of smell like stinky feet! Some of the same bacteria that's used to make the cheese is also found on the human foot.

I wash my feet—a lot. And I change my
shoes. Then I race back outside.
And guess what. . . .

The mosquitoes don't like me as much as before! "Look, only one bite!" I tell my friends.

"We solved the mosquito mystery!" says Lara.

"Yeah," says Steve. "But I'll kind of miss watching Riley trying to shoo them away."

I do the mosquito dance one last time, just for Steve. What are friends for?

So mosquitoes are after you, and you don't have stinky feet? It could be your breath, your sweat, your hairspray — even a full moon.... Or maybe mosquitoes just like you!

I can test!

THINK LIKE A SCIENTIST

Mosquitoes are bugging Riley! So he investigates to find out why. Then he tests out his ideas.

Scientists do tests, too. (One scientist even wore the same socks for three days straight, just to see if mosquitoes liked the smell!)

Look Back

- Look at page 7. What does Riley observe about the mosquitoes? What question does he ask? What idea does he test out on page 8?
- What does Riley test on page 13? Does it work?
- Riley has another idea on page 29. How does he test it? Is the test successful? Explain your thoughts.

Try This!

The kids in these pictures are making tests. Say what you think they're trying to find out. What do you think the results will be?

1. 2.

Fruity Patootie   Mix!   Choco-Chunk

Possible answers: 1. She is testing how plants will grow in the sun and in the dark. 2. She is testing how the mixed flavors will taste.